Reading Like A Girl

Reading Like A Girl

Rishma Dunlop

Black Moss Press
2004

National Library of Canada Cataloguing in Publication

Dunlop, Rishma, 1956-
        Reading like a girl / Rishma Dunlop.

Poems.
ISBN 0-88753-396-5

        I. Title.

PS8557.U53995R43 2004   C811'.6   C2004-901867-1

Published by Black Moss Press at 2450 Byng Road, Windsor, Ontario
N8W 3E8. Black Moss books are distributed in Canada and the U.S. by
Firefly Books, Firefly Books Ltd., 66 Leek Crescent, Richmond Hill,
ON Canada L4B 1H1. All orders should be directed there.

Black Moss would like to acknowledge the generous support to its
publishing program from the Canada Council and the Ontario Arts
Council for its publishing program.

ONTARIO ARTS COUNCIL
CONSEIL DES ARTS DE L'ONTARIO

Le Conseil des Arts | The Canada Council
du Canada | for the Arts

Late have I loved you,
O beauty so ancient and so new.
                              —Augustine: Confessions 10, 27

Publication Credits

The Blue Hour, LyricalMyrical Press, 2004.
The Body of My Garden, Mansfield Press, 2002.
Boundary Bay, Staccato/Turnstone, 2000.

My thanks to the editors of the following publications in which these poems appeared in earlier versions:
Windsor Review "Gathering Lilacs," "Cartography," "Slow Dancing: Beaconsfield 1973."
Niagara Current "Theology."
The Comstock Review "Anthem," Honorable Mention, Muriel Craft Bailey Prize.
Canadian Literature "Psalm for the Beloved."
Body Language: A Head To Toe Anthology, Black Moss Press 2003, "Memento Mori."
Leaving Footsteps: An Anthology of Southern Ontario Women Poets, Black Moss Press 2004, "Slow Burn."
Language and Literacy, "Angelus Novus," " Strange Fruit," "The Lost Language of Cranes," "Somewhere, a woman is writing a poem."
Descant "First Lessons, Postcolonial, "My Mother's Lost Places"
Changing English "Lector in Fabula," "Reading Like a Girl," "Reading Amy Lowell."
ARM "Reading Chekhov," "The Education of Girls."

Contents

Saccade

The chronicle of the city unravels
                    like a prayer cloth
calm of storybook nurseries, book codes,
swift calligraphy of desire.

The city dreams us
              gives us exigencies in eavesdropped
              stories, undistinguished pleadings
              requiems for forgetting.

There is a small star pinned where Hiroshima used to be.

It's late and someone's almost forgotten how to convince you
                              he's telling the truth.
Even in sleep he cries out for help
              and you minister to him
              a woman like history returning for its wounded.

Blackbirds drop from telephone wires
                        rosepetals collect in birdbaths.

                ————

Everything stories you. You take Rilke at his word
Taste it everywhere. Wonderland signs
                    Eat me. Drink me.

Your hands like hobbled birds
read the classics. The hero enters the arched gate of the city.
In these books it is clear where the story of the city begins.

In the book of lost entries
                    nothing is pure but the forgotten things
crossed out words on a haunted page
                                        useless dark of ink.

———

Today the city is unwriting itself
                    in a coffin of glass.

In the blurred doorways,
                    in skyscrapers that rise silver and blue
cool as if nothing could ever make them burn.

Sprayed on concrete walls
Where is my beautiful daughter
Emma was here
Escúchame
I'll pray for you Lucas
Fuck the politicians
Recuérdame
Inamorata

the billboard with the women tall
                    with long legs against white sand and blue ocean
                    red mouths puckered high above the crowds
smooth lipsticked smiles longing for cigarettes and sex.

———

Across the city, lights are shutting off
Good night, good night.

On the radio, the sirens are singing
Emily Lou Harris, Alison Kraus, Gillian Welch
ethereal lullaby *Didn't Leave Nobody But the Baby*

Come lay your bones
on the alabaster stones
and be my ever-lovin' baby.

Reading Emily Dickinson
                    Beauty crowds me til I die.
You feel the loneliness.
That's what is left of the dream of beauty.

Beauty
        So many kinds to name.

You hope for a day soft at the edges
                    for something, someone to
                    know the small hands of rain
to be like rain
wet with a decent happiness.

———

Kiss the gleaming armor of the world.
Feel its electric purr.
Close your hands on wind-stunned leaves.
Buff the scars of history with your mouth.

Primer

The girl reads neighbourhoods of
dog, cat, sister, brother, mother, father
houses lit with yellow sunshine and once
upon a time glass slippers, long-toothed wolves.

———

The girl does not know yet
                the broken world,
that there will be pages for *consequence, coercion, fraudulence.*

Outside her room
the sky is an X-Ray pinned to light
             armies of birds lifting into skeletal shadows.
Softness vanishes in the city
             deformed by *contagion, fear, vanity.*

News stories convulse
             palsied in the laws of speech.
Planes pass over the skyline.
Traffic lights change voltage.
Damage is quiet
            oil slick pools in city parkades
fissured winds, smudge of newsprint.
Elegant hands read the book of lost entries
         trace the red glares of exit signs, writing on tenement walls
                  the veined arms of junkies.

———

The girl reads her picture books.
A child's garden of verses.
The alphabet sifts into her ribcage
                    opens her to stars, grass, abcs
whole sentences whispering dark.

In the open doorway
                something cold and distant
even adult hands are small against it.

The book left on the lectern
brittle yellow pages without context
                        lexicons of disclosure
soft imprisonment.

The girl does not know yet how words will
                    hiss and tremble on fuller pages
imagined wilderness, insomniac's tale, seductions,
remembrances and forgettings, child's face pressed
against shattered window, wrecked lullaby, fiercely beautiful
derailment, murderer's knife, deep song of
mouth unnaming the known.

———

My hands close on empty testimonies
                until I find that girl—a pocket of held light
ripped corner of one illuminated manuscript.

In my dreams I see her
the pages blowing with dormant
                          terror
as she gathers moon and sky
in her small hands like a mouth lovely language
that has no word for *harm*.

Alphabet

Angel he calls me, *angel* says the
Boy on the street when I give him a dollar.
Choreography everywhere in the city,
            crows wheeling and dancing on the horizon,   every cell recalls
Desire, Billie Holiday's *distingué* lovers, slick, slippery memories of
Evenings drunk with stars and rain and
Frank Sinatra crooning love letters like
Grace notes in the summer air.
Heat hisses on the boulevards
Inches over our skins like imagined sighs and opium smoke.
Jack Kerouac screams out angel! on a midnight moving train.
Kisses for the junkies eating oranges.
Love a one word intangible cipher
Many-mouthed birds sing *Kyrie Eleison*
Nocturnes and nightingales
Open wide the hearts of the innocent and the not-so-innocent.
Pink the colour of Ginger Rogers' shoes turned
pink with blood
                  after Fred asks for hundreds of takes for a single scene.
Queers and transvestite divas dance in the street in a costume parade.
Ruined beauty. We can always be romantic and pray for its return.
Stubbornness is underrated. It spines us,
Threading us through the lives of those we barely know
Until each of us becomes the ash and bone of the other.
Vanity tricks us until the collapse on bloody feet
When hobo skies dream us into adventures of comic-book heroes with
X-ray vision,   new gods of the city
Yawping across skyscrapers and apartment buildings
Zest of their goodness like an absolute tasted on the wind.

Gathering Lilacs

Every street is a confluence
of dreams, of lips to stars.
Everywhere I travel there is still this—
a small girl in her red dress.
Her father clasps her hand in his, teaches her
the convulsive beauty of things
as they walk through the garden
gathering flowers.

All her days she wanders
the sacred, the strange, through lost altars.
All her days she longs for the thing
that would fill her life.

In the heat-stoned afternoon
the air is drenched with the scent of lilacs.
I cut bunches loose with kitchen shears
quench them
in every available vase and bowl, arrange
them on sills, and mantles and ledges.

At midnight I gather armfuls for you,
place them on the bed, tuck them between
sheets, lay them against the rough of your
cheek, against the veins of your sleeping eyelids
as I finish your dreams.

These days every street leads me
to you, where love is negligent,
laying bare everything
recognition rustling in leaves.

Augustinian Heart

We talk about art and its source
                              of greatness.
How a painting or poem could move you like
a religious impulse, spirit and matter infused,
                              true and beautiful.
Year after year each time you read that poem, or
see that painting, a still-life, a self-portrait,
                              an abstract landscape so loved by the artist
you ache to touch it, to hold it.

————

We talk into the night.
Behind the house, the crescent moon silvers
                              the wilderness dark.
In the flesh of my hand—the knowledge of your flesh:
                              all I need; all I know.

If art is a private religion, so is love. We take it all to heart,
as if, Augustine said, our existence depends upon our having loved.
Beauty so ancient and so new.

We try to tell each other about the sacred
                              what needs to be visible to the jaded eye.

————

The long slow walk leads us back to each other.
Winter air frosts our bones and our cold arms are full
of each other and the everyday immortal ache of spirit for matter,
                              of matter for spirit.
I have come to understand this is the same need
grasped through the lips   hands   body and in the
vision that if we touch what we love, if we hold it,
                              behold it, then it will last.

Anthem

1

Place your hands that I love upon me.
Say my name as prayer. Taste each
brine sweet syllable. This is what will
haunt us. Stone hearts in our mouths.
Your love will not be salvation.
This I know.

2

Watch me burn. The cells of my old body
melt away. Bracelet my wrists with your grip.
Drink the blue that rivers my hands. Make my bones
lovely.

3

Meet the rush of my wants, meet the
light of outrage, the after-burn. Edgelit.

4

Language is always culpable. Grammar
a climate of love. Write in the colors of a
Tintoretto dusk. Slice of moon, scrape of sky,
armfuls of rain. Read me with conviction, absolute.
Fit your words to me like the precise cut
of tuxedo, riding jacket, Dior gown.

5

Take every journey into the past,
delusions, false namings of events.
Take memory that gnaws on the ribs and
turn it into prophecy. Revise me until brave
new days bloom in my throat.

6

Love me. Cradle me in gentleness.
Release the heart's shroud. Make me the
last poem in your book. Let me hear you say
I want this more than anything. This love will
not save us. I would run from it but it is the
only grace. *Love. Lean into its slant.* Postscript
of light in every century.

Petitions to Heaven

Pale chapel of sky over Central Park.
At the Guggenheim Museum in the exhibit of Brazilian
art are the ex-votos, called milagros, miracles. Carvings of
wooden body parts: feet, arms, legs, eyes, breasts, hearts. Each
milagro a petition to the saints to mend a fractured leg,
a broken heart.

And I travel back to that spring in New Mexico,
you and I under Ave Maria skies, impossible
light meeting the pink adobe and desert horizon.
That day in the heart of the Gila Forest, after the rains,
thousands of hummingbirds part the air, speeding flying jewels,
joyas voladoras, blurred wing-beats from feeders to flowers, these
flower-kissers, messengers from the gods.

There was the woman
wearing a stuffed hummingbird
as amulet around her neck, a lucky
charm for matters of the heart, the
dried heart ground into powder for
love potions.

She tells us the Apache legend of
Wind Dancer, the young deaf warrior
who sang magical, wordless songs that
brought good weather and healing.

He loved a woman named Bright Rain.

When Wind Dancer dies tragically, the
world is plunged into bitter winter. Until
one day Bright Rain begins to take solitary
walks in the forest and spring returns.
Wind Dancer returns to her in the form of a
hummingbird, dressed in the bright
ceremonial costume of a warrior
in fields of flowers where he
would whisper secrets to his beloved.

***

We have petitioned heaven, you and I, asking for some silver thread from
earth to sky to guide us, to unravel some logic for our dreams of angels.

Here, the wind from the arroyo drapes our eyelids with tribal
silver, lights our way with *farolitos* and paper lanterns,
paints my toes matador red, tongues us in Spanish love:
mi bien querido, te quiero, mi corazón.

In you, the weight of rain bursting, the scent of chaos in your clothes.
Nights of love in the desert, your mouth becomes midnight, becomes dawn.

***

Fiesta Sunday.
The Virgin of Assisi is carried in procession.
La Conquistadora, she is called, three feet tall, stern-faced.
Mass in the cathedral, children from the Santa Clara Pueblo, dancing.
The Mariachi band sings a hymn: De Colores:
Y por eso los grandes amores
De muchos colores me gustan a mi

La Conquistadora gazes over us. Women, men, children, line up
to touch her, to kiss the hem of her blue velvet cloak embroidered
with stars and edged in silver, the cross around her neck gleaming.
One by one, they pin tiny *milagros* to her garments, silver and gold hands
and feet, hearts, arms, legs.

On this day, at a Mass with strangers, their rituals and angels and gods
strange to us, spirit is a thread knotted to the gristle of our bodies.
You are growing old in me. I'll be the one who closes your eyes.
The air, thick with prayers, promises your winged return.

We kiss that velvet hem, pin our fragile hearts there.

Notes from a Journal

Read Dante. Continue to tell me that Beatrice is spelled like my name in your heart. Shift the ground in your touch. Let the hand of love shape my throat into singing. Give me poetry as *sacra conversacione* no borders between lips and ears. *Love is my weight.* Let me feel your kiss raw through the scraped bones of the past, through the shiver of history. Be for me like the saxophone of John Coltrane, thrumming my spine. Be like the voice of honey, Nina Simone singing *I want a little sugar in my bowl.* Rough my hand with your tongue. Embroider my skin with constellations. Soften the sharp things of the world.

Angelus Novus

Glorious autumnal skies. Cathedrals of light.
First day of classes at the university.
In another city an uncertain wind howls into dissonance.
It is not the faces of my students I remember that day, but
the sheer and immense futility of speech. My words
stones in my throat. How to teach about literature,
about poetry, when the book opens to such a page,
blackened by the charred wings of the angel of history.

After this eleventh day in September, there are those
fashioning crosses from twigs, praying to angels with persistence.
It is not the faces of the victims that haunt me, nor the ruined avenues,
nor the steel towers in flame. Not the widows' anguish. Not the
violinist on the front page of the newspaper, tears streaming
down her face as she plays a fugue. Not the powdered bone or seared
flesh, not the face of hatred.

It is the shoes that I remember, the shoes that haunt me, falling
everywhere like rain from the towers, people running out of their
shoes, rows of firemen's boots abandoned, a woman's high heel,
everywhere shoes in smoldering ash, full lives still hissing
O remember me I walked here. This speech of common steps
propelling us into the future.

I can say nothing. What can I say—that darkness reveals beauty?
That terror will yield clear-sight? I cannot stand at
a lectern—professing.

Yet with them in classrooms day after day, I am trying to write
something that recalls beauty to the mortal, the imperfect,
the guilty. Something that speaks of stars falling on the city,
that is dream-cut, embossed onto cream-laid papers, my poem for them,
born of remembrances of those ashen footprints vanishing from the air.

Something that would allow us all to die in full desire.
Something that would calm the stormwinds blowing in from Paradise.
Something that would heal those scorched wings, allow the angel to
close them, fold them gently back into
the dark waters of our hearts.

Lector in Fabula

I am reading in a school of dreams,
a lost girl in a night's tale, wandering through
a *jardin d'essais,* underfoot, the crunch of pale
green lichen on the forest floor.

Hyacinth gardens fade into a scene of
city lights and I am on Vancouver's Hastings Street.
The pages become stained with east end rot, humanity
pumping heroin through collapsed veins and
there on the corner is a woman weeping, the sound of
her pain palpable in every crack of concrete,
a prostitute whose knees have been broken by
a man with a baseball bat. I take her by the hand and
take her home with me, wash her body and her crushed limbs,
her sore-covered feet. I try to absorb her fever in my touch,
lay her down to sleep in my bed.

In the morning when I wake, she is gone,
only a cool, clear light shining on the tumbled sheets.

Tonight, I'll turn the pages of the book again
my hands inside the spine, reading the places
where memory doesn't work.

The Reader

after the Gerhard Richter painting, "Lesende" (Reader),
oil on linen, 1994

The artist claims to paint beauty
for its own sake.

She enters the painting
precise as a photograph
every pore of the woman's skin
ponytail at her nape
golden O of earring
tension of neck and hands
as she reads the newspaper with its text
unreadable, and then the woman blurs
to ghost, her moment already past in history.

First Lessons: Postcolonial

Every morning my mother would
part my hair down the middle, plait
it into long braids reaching down to
my waist. I would walk with the other
neighbourhood kids to Briarwood Elementary
School, absent-minded, face always
in a book, reading as I walked, dressed like
the other girls in dark navy tunics, white blouses,
novitiate-like collars.

Those days, my knees were always scraped
and skinned from roller-skating on the concrete
slopes of Avondale Road, my skate-keys around
my neck, flying, weightless
my father continuously swabbing my cuts with
hydrogen peroxide, scabs peeking out over the
tops of white kneesocks, my Oxford shoes.

In class, we stood at attention
spines stiffened to the strains of singing
God Save the Queen to the Union Jack
recited The Lord's Prayer
hallowed be thy name, learned lessons
from a Gideon's bible.

In geography and history lessons the
teacher would unroll the giant map of
the world from the ceiling, use her

wooden pointer to show the countries
of the Empire, the slow spread of a faded
red stain that marked them, soft burgundy
like the colour of my father's turbans.
Ancient history. Crisp whites of cricket
matches at officers' clubs. Afternoon tea
in the pavilion.

Decades later I can reconstruct the
story, move past the pink glow,
excavate the hollows of history.

If that surface was scratched
the pointer would fly along the contours of
the parchment world, across the Himalayas,
through emerald coils of steaming rivers.
Under my fingernails, the scents of spices
and teas, the silk phrasings of my mother's
saris, the stench of imperial legacy, blood
spilled from swords on proper khaki uniforms
lanced through the bodies of Sikh soldiers at
the frontlines of her Majesty's British Army.

But our teacher never said. *Remember this.*

My Mother's Lost Places

My teachers and the women in the
neighbourhood would admire the crimson
blooms on my mother's Kashmiri shawls,
exotic, intricate embroideries on the finest
wool the colour of nightfall.

I know they could never imagine,
as I have only just begun to imagine,
my mother's lost places,
laughter in summer houses, wild monkeys
at the hill stations of her youth, peacocks,
the heady profusions of flowers and fruit,
jasmine and roses, custard-apples and
guavas. They could not imagine her with
braids and proper Catholic uniform at the
convent school under the stern eyes of nuns
with their Bride of Christ wedding rings
who taught them all their subjects including
domestic skills such as the tatting of lace and
embroidery stitching. They could not taste the
sweetness of Sanskrit poetry, or the star-flung
nights of Persian ghazals.

In Canada, my mother's young life gets frozen into
the icy winters of my childhood, new stories spun
in English on skating rinks, tobogganing hills and
ski slopes. A new wife, a new mother, she reads
Ladies Home Journal, learns to bake me birthday
cakes and gingerbread houses, wears Western clothes,
pedal pushers and sheath dresses and high heels, sews
me party frocks with sashes bowed in the back.

The Education of Girls

We learn to recite the Girl Guide promise:

I promise, on my honour, to do my best:
To do my duty to God, the Queen, and my country,
To help other people at all times,
To obey the Guide Law.

We learn the language of semaphore, how to
build campfires and lean-tos and latrines. We earn
badges, pitch tents, learn how to use an axe and chop wood,
how to tie knots, learn first aid and how to survive in the
wilderness. We learn to *Be Prepared* and to *Lend a Hand.*

We learn the Guide Law.

A Guide is obedient. You obey orders given you by those
in authority, willingly and quickly. Learn to understand that
orders are given for a reason, and must be carried out without question.

A Guide smiles and sings even under difficulty. You are
cheerful and willing even when things seem to be going wrong.

A Guide is pure in thought, word and deed. You look for
what is beautiful and good in everything, and try to become strong
enough to discard the ugly and unpleasant.

We become capable girls, soldiers in our uniforms, with our
companies and patrols and salutes. We learn to build nations and
at the close of the day, we sing Taps, the soldiers' bugle call to
extinguish the lights.

Day is done, gone the sun
From the hills, from the lake
From the sky
All is well, safely rest
God is nigh.

And our mothers kept house, did laundry and
cooking and ironing,
did volunteer work, refinished furniture,
watched *The Edge of Night* and *Another World*
took Valium when their lives did
not resemble the glamorous adventures of Rachel
and Mac Corey, had hysterectomies at 40.
At the close of every day, they had supper ready when
their husbands returned from the city, fresh and slick,
briefcases in hand, polished shoes tapping them home past
manicured lawns along the asphalt driveways.

Reading Like a Girl: 1

First stories, fragments of colonial texts,
Enid Blyton, Noddy's adventures, Kipling's *Jungle Book*
Wordsworth's daffodils
stories full of words like pram, lorry, Wellingtons, nappies.

Then worlds of fairies and witches
Rapunzel letting down her hair from the tower,
princesses and ogres.

The story she loved best was Little Red Riding Hood.
As a young child she learned all the words
                                    by heart.
In the storybook her parents read to her,
Little Red is always saved by the woodcutter.

Years later, when she knows the real ending, the Perrault
one where the wolf waits for her in bed, and Little Red takes off
her clothes, lies down beside him and he gobbles her up
                                    it is no surprise.

She is still the red cloaked one, using her words as incantations
against the wolf at the door, the wolf who comes again and again
                                    on nights black as doctrine.

There is no other story, no other text.

Reading Like a Girl: 2

The comic book heroes I loved best
                              were the mutants and freaks.
Spiderman and Batman, Aquaman who was half-fish.

And then there was Wonder Woman. She was glorious,
descended from the Amazons of Greek myth. She had
fabulous breasts, a tiara, a magic lasso and belt, red boots,
as well as those bulletproof wristbands worn by the
Amazons to remind them of the folly of submitting to men's domination.
If a man could bind an Amazon's wrists, she lost all her powers.

In early stories she captures
spies, Third World War Promoters,
sends them to imprisonment on Venus
where they are forced to wear
Venus Girdles of Magnetic Gold to
tame them into peaceful life.
In another story, she defeats the
evil Fausta, Nazi Wonder Woman
in "Wanted by Hitler, Dead or Alive."

Wonder Woman was beautiful and powerful as a hero,
understated and reserved in her secret identity as Diana Prince,
the secretary in her smart-chick glasses.

She taught me radical truth.
The geek, the hybrid mutant is a treasure,
so easily misunderstood in real life
a secret identity is necessary. Hold it close.
Protect your wrists.
Put on your red boots   step into fire.

Reading Like a Girl: 3

Reading my mother's magazines
Ladies Home Journal and *Miss Chatelaine*
pictures of women with cinch-waist dresses,
bouffant hairdos. They ride in convertibles
headscarves keeping every hair in place.

These women are so happy with their pink and aqua
kitchen appliances. In one ad for Scott toilet paper,
the woman wears an evening gown in the exact
pastel blue of the toilet paper and Kleenex tissue.

These women use Yardley Lavender and Cashmere Bouquet
talcum powder. They buy new davenports and credenzas. Pictured
in exotic landscapes in their underwear, they dream in their Maidenform
bras and girdles that promise to set them free.

The ad I like best is for the black lace corset called a Merry Widow.
Under the sedate hairdo and perfect makeup of the model,
her Max Factor red lips whisper
It's simply wicked what it does for you.
Care to be daring, darling?

Reading Like a Girl: 4

At our school, girls are separated from
boys, gathered in the school gymnasium.
The nurse distributes pamphlets about
life cycles and Kotex. There is something
pristine and sanitized about it, the glossy
brochures with the beautiful fresh-faced
girl, blonde hair swept back with pink
satin ribbon. We read all about this girl and
know we will soon become her, young women
                              leading Breck girl lives.

We learn our lessons well, believe we can
hold on to our well-groomed dreams.

It takes us years before we realize how many
things will make us bleed, how easy
for the world to rip us to pieces.

Reading Like a Girl : 5

Long after my mother thought I was asleep,
late into the night, I would read under the
covers with a flashlight.

How I loved them, the stories about the
girl detectives, reading and recording the
world in notebooks—Harriet the Spy
the ones who solved crimes with their
wits, their brains, their All-American good looks.

I drove that blue roadster with Nancy
Drew, dated Ned, looked lovely and charming
and desirable at college football games.

And how I dreamed of being Cherry Ames, student
nurse, with her stylish cap and uniform, her black
hair and rosy cheeks, her boyfriends and her adventures.

And when I grew up, I became them, Nancy and Cherry.
I cut off my long black braids, styled my hair into a bob.

I became the girl detective, the nurse, capable of building
nations and soothing the hearts of men
for awhile.

Reading Like A Girl : 6

The volume of Tolstoy thumbs her open.
She tries to keep the heroine alive.

Outside the library windows
ragged moths beat against the streetlamps.
She feels the heat of locomotive steam
rising from the stacks, weeps when she
sees Anna's red purse on the tracks.

She closes the book with stunned hands
as if she had touched the hem of a final
morning, a sense of that going into it alone.
She begins to think she will not be carried
unscarred, untorn into any heaven. Wants
someone to hold her while she burns.

Slow Dancing: Beaconsfield 1973

Parents away for the weekend
we are in a house like all the others,
freshly painted trim and gabled windows,
brass-numbered door and neatly pruned hedges,
and the basement recreation room is overflowing
with us, sweet sixteens, bodies clutched together in sweat in
the cigarette smoke and beer, slow dancing to Chicago's *Color
My World* and Led Zeppelin's *Stairway to Heaven.*

My girlfriends and I wear angora sweaters our mothers
bought for us in the soft pastel shades of infants: fingernail
pink, baby blue, pale yellow, and cream. We wear drugstore
scents named for innocence and fruit: *Love's Baby Soft, Love's Fresh
Lemon,* or the more sophisticated *Eau de Love* or Revlon's *Charlie.*

For years we have danced in ballet studios, spinning, dreaming our mothers'
dreams of Sugar Plum Fairies, our rose tight confections, pink slippers twirling
pas de deux, jetés, pirouetting our taut muscles until our toes bled. But tonight
we dance in our tight blue Levis, our mothers' voices fading as Eric Clapton's
electric guitar shivers our spines, the music claiming us and we spill out
under the streetlamps, dancing across equators into the earth's light.

On the streets of suburbia, this is the beginning of hunger.
It catches me by surprise, exploding like a kiss.

Princess Stories

When I was young my father called me *Princess*.
And princess stories were the ones I loved most,
especially the one about Sleeping Beauty. Her
name was sometimes Briar Rose or Aurora. The
story of the beautiful princess who pricked her
finger on the spindle of a spinning wheel, falling
under the spell of the witch who had been shunned
at her christening. The curse of a girlchild's birth.

She slept along with her kingdom for a hundred years
until she is rescued by a handsome prince who hacked
through the dense tangle of thorn and wild roses.
The curse lifted with love, his kiss on her lips
awakened the world.

While my daughters are young, I read them princess stories
The Paper Bag Princess, The Princess and the Motorcycle.
tales of strong, independent princesses of wit and courage and
intellect who do not depend on princes.

Still, as I watch my girls, young women now, I am filled
with longing, something that mourns the loss of belief
that a beloved would hack through forests of thorns into
waking.

Soja

In my parents' bedroom
the bureau holds the gifts he gave her,
lingerie drawers of lace and silk, peignoir sets of filmy chiffon,
bottles of perfume *Chanel No.5, Miss Dior, Je Reviens.*

Silver-framed photographs on the nightstand,
lives stilled in sepia and Kodachrome.
There we are, the three of us on Parliament Hill among
tulips, my mother in her red sari, red shoes, red handbag,
my father with his turban, me in my British duffle coat with
the pointed hood, blue like the one Paddington bear wore.

Another snapshot.
My father teaching me to skate on Rideau Canal,
to lie in fresh powder and make snow angels.

In this one I am walking with my mother
in the Gatineau Hills in the flame of maple trees.
We are dressed to match our new country,
my mother in orange printed sari
me in my orange frock sashed at my waist.

A handtinted photo. My mother in her 50's bathing suit,
posing in front of the rounded curves of our blue Ford.
Coke bottles cooling in the sand, lined up along the shoreline.

There is my mother in her sari in front of Niagara Falls.
In another shot the three of us are standing under the falls
                                    in our shiny yellow slickers.

I know the gleam and smell of the polished
leather of his shoes, buffed every morning
                                    before he left for work.
I press my face into the crisp white cotton of his shirts,
brush my cheek against his jackets,
sweaters still warm with him.
I touch my teeth to the metal of his watch, his cufflinks.

I can hear his voice reading fairytales, singing
Harry Belafonte's " Jamaica Farewell"

But I'm sad to say I'm on my way
Won't be back for many a day
My heart is down, my head is turning around
I had to leave a little girl in Kingston town

I hear him singing Punjabi and Hindi ghazals, lullabies

Soja Rajkumari, soja,
Soja meethe sapne aayen
Soja pyari Rajkumari

Sleep, princess, sleep
Sleep with sweet dreams
Sleep beloved princess

In the hush, I am cradled by the sound of him,
voice lifting me like birdsong through the pyre.

In my mother's house I enter silence,
wear it as a dress, my father's ashes acrid
in my throat. I remember the days of savage
adoration, child for father, father for child, when
I was tiny enough to stick to his trousers like a burr.
His sudden vanishing a brute sledgehammer blow.

Reading Amy Lowell

Summer and I have returned to the town where
                                        I was a young wife
where we raised our daughters.
The name of the place means *a place to live forever.*
Mythology and daily life. Legends of sea serpents,
ghosts of horses lost swimming in from the island, tangled with
slow pitch tournaments, ball players and Winnebago campers,
tourists on the beaches and lunching at wineries.

Today I am marking freshman English papers in the backyard.
The air is sweet and fugitive. In the garden, wild strew of roses,
pink blooms amidst the silver foliage of planted pathways
                                fragrance spilling from their thorn beds
the morning stillness stung by the
screeching of Steller's jays and flocks of crows
                                singing a crude chorale.

In the distance, the sound of ducks landing on the swimming pool,
                                splashing and flapping their wings.
My daughters laugh and I am struck by that particular radiance
                        again and again   how the laughter of girls
                                cuts through blue air.

How did I come to this place
                                the professor circling sentence fragments,
the occasional leap of the heart when a student writes a beautiful phrase.
My student has written an essay on Amy Lowell.
And suddenly I am transported, back to 1972 at Beaconsfield High
in Mr. Whitman's North American Literature class,
                                        yes that was his name.

Fifteen years old, sitting in those straight-backed wooden chairs,
my legs cramped under the tiny desk with my huge Norton anthology
                              open at Amy Lowell's "Patterns."
There have been so many poems I have committed to heart.
          This poem was one of them.
I could taste this poetry, feel the rhythms of it beating in my eyelids.
For the first time, reading Amy Lowell,
              I understood that burnt cadence of sense,
                        the quickstep of syllables in my throat.

I wrote an essay on Amy Lowell's "Patterns"
something about the Imagist movement, the poet's use of figurative
                              language and form
in a consideration of how societal expectations may
                        inhibit a woman's actions in society.

Mr. Whitman gave me an A on my essay.

I promptly forgot what I knew about patterns
                        in the wisdom of my sixteenth year.

I must have known then, something about the effect of patterns,
knowing Lowell's narrator, the feel of her corset, her pink and silver
brocade gown, how she grieves for her dead lover
                    how a heavy-booted lover would have loosened
                        the stays of her stiff correct brocade
in the pink and silver garden
                        the bruise and swoon of it.

I too am a rare
Pattern.

In dreams I see the husband of my girlhood
                              my pink and silver time
his arms around me like a familiar blanket.
He is holding something out to me, places it in my palm
              a scroll, a tablet, some lost history inscribed
                                        unreadable.

And centuries pass and we are still *gorgeously arrayed*
                              trousseaus of pink and silver
mouths stuffed with bone china
pink and silver, boned and stayed

Christ! What are patterns for?

At sixteen I used to mouth the words
                              swords springing from the repetitions
from the ribs of consonants.

Today, in my forty-sixth year, I reread the poem and the body flies apart,
remembering how a grown woman can brush back her hair in moonlight
watch her husband and daughters inside her house as if in a dream.

Remembering days when the woman wakes up and she understands her skin
doesn't fit her anymore.

What she does inside that skin leaves
                     her outside her house in long nights of crickets
                              singing and the lake whispering.

Sometimes, she longs to be like characters in a novel or a poem,
                             the relief of flatness on paper.

The heart is literate.
                   It wants to read the pages it has unfurled.
It wants the grip of roses on love-ridden afternoons,

                   the ordinary of tv, chair, table, plate, sneakers
entangled through a sky of blood tracery swept innocent by rain.

I want conversation that is like the stripped truth of the poem,
the way I felt when I first read Amy Lowell's "Patterns."
Over the years I wondered what kind of shelter
                           I could make with words.
I search for the color of home in the extravagance of reading.
I am looking for it still.

This town is not a place for introspection. Such beauty.
The lake, the blue air, the sun, all defy me
                      to find some fault in this horizon.

Over the years I weaned my babies, got ready to walk
                      into the pink and silver light.

Reading Chekhov

Reading Chekhov. Stories about love
   the sadness of his characters, always meeting each other too late.
Missed lives, mourning what could have been
                    departing forever in railway stations.
Tears, a lorgnette raised to the eye, ice etched on windows,
            gaslit winter scenes
                    a loveless marriage in a country house in a town
                    like all the others.

I'll read the story differently. A Chekhov love letter.

Love me through departures,
through the faltering valves of your heart,
                    the ticking of clocks and moving trains.

Kiss me in the cleft of each elbow, behind each knee.

                    ———

Buddhists tell us to live our days unattached
                            to the dust of the world
                                to enter the blackness.
To always see ourselves as light.

Not so easy to do when the hum of the world
                            dulls us in its gears.
I am trying to wear light as a garment
                to find it in the paradise of afterlife under a stone
                in the opened door of a commuter train.

———

Departure lounge at the airport.
Goodbye a salt-water word you avoid
        as if it would open a wound that would never close.
Goodbye a word of red waves, fog-horn sobs, sea-wracked,
        tongue-uttered ache
        ember of pain in the wrist, a movement toward
        the corrosive heart.
Goodbye a word that makes your bones scream a word you dare not
breathe.

———

I am always naked with you.
The winds brought me newborn into your arms
        to the one who would hold me through the night.

I have always known you.
        My harsh blessing.
Every sweetness has the taste of your skin.
Each wound has the shape of your mouth.

Forget me. As I would forget you. For the suffering.

Remember me. As I would remember you. Claim the way the heart stops
when you come to me naked and scratched.
Climb to my bed bleeding
        on the dark wind of dreams.

———

I have waited for you all my life.
Four decades to find you
                    and still and still a story that turns back on itself.

Dance with me beloved.
                    I am your wild, sweet girl.
I would have you as you are,
                    aging and heartsick with the world.

                    ———

All night, all night you can have this book.
Turn the pages on your lap, until they become like well-worn linen
last words soft in your hands.

Meet me there in that story
afterlife of spine cracked open.

The Lost Language of Cranes

I

For if Hiroshima in the morning, after the bomb has fallen,
Is like a dream, one must ask whose dream it is.
Peter Schwenger, *Letter Bomb: Nuclear Holocaust and the Exploding Word*

1

Reading with my daughter
the story of *Sadako and the Thousand Cranes.*
Rachel loves to tell the story
of the little Japanese girl who is almost two when the
bomb explodes a mile from her home in Hiroshima.
They run, fleeing to the banks of the River Ota
drenched by the black rain,
falling, falling.

When she is twelve years old,
Sadako runs like the wind in school relay races
best runner in the sixth grade, until she falters
her body gnawed away by leukemia,
Atomic Bomb Disease.

In the hospital, her friends remind her
of the *Tsuru,* the crane
Japanese symbol of long life, of hope.
If you fold a thousand cranes.
they will protect you from illness,
grant you a wish.

Sadako tells the cranes
I will write peace on your wings
and you will fly all over the world
Sadako begins folding,
folding fragments of newspapers,
discarded wrappers from her medicines,
making tiny paper cranes,
folding, folding

Sadako's mother writes:
If she has to suffer like this,
she should have died that morning
on August 6th.

She watches her daughter, her
painstaking folding.
She buys a bolt of silk fabric
printed with cherry blossoms,
makes a kimono to enfold her child.
Sadako's small fingers folding,
folding day after day.

She makes 644 cranes before she dies.
Her classmates complete her thousand cranes,
place them in her coffin,
as if her heart would continue to beat in the paper wings.

Her mother wraps her daughter
in the softness of silk,
in the cherry blossom kimono,

lays flowers in the coffin with the birds, so that her child
can bring them with her to the next world.
Sadako's mother asks the birds:
Why didn't you sing? Why didn't you fly?

2

A cemetery seen from the air is a child's city.
Carolyn Forché, *"The Garden Shukkei-en"*

I watch my daughter and her friends
folding tiny origami cranes for their class project,
winged symbols of peace, spread rainbow-hued
across the kitchen table.

The paper birds criss-cross the earth
correspondences for peace projects,
their hopeful wings trying to speak
the horrors of war amidst the cheery optimism
of chalkboards and classrooms.

The children will send the paper cranes
in garlands of a hundred birds each
to the mayor of Hiroshima,
to be placed with millions of paper cranes
at the foot of the Children's Monument where the stone figure
of Sadako
holds a large golden crane above her head,
arms outstretched to the sky.

I watch my children play and wonder
if the power of birds will stand strong against
exploding words and mushroom clouds
against the screams that reverberate
in the silence of Hiroshima's Peace Park.

3

After I noticed the flash, white clouds spread over the blue sky.
It was as if blue morning glories had suddenly bloomed...
Testimony of Isao Kita

By the banks of the river Ota,
where Sadako used to play in the Garden Shukkei-en,
stands a stone angel holding an origami crane.
Hibakusha, survivors who are still alive
wander the garden, across the pond
on the Kokoukyo Bridge, through tea ceremonies
and the blossomings of plums and cherries and irises.

In the garden, the silence,
the insistence of memory, the flash of light,
the burning heat, the shattering of glass,
everywhere the cries of children calling for
their mothers.

Bodies stripped naked by the
blast, skin peeling, hanging from fingertips

like cloth, mothers holding dying children
in their arms, trying in vain to pluck away
the swarming maggots.
Bones in rice bowls,
babies crawling over dead mothers, rooting for
nipples, seeking milk, their reflections shimmering
like ghosts.

Against a clear blue sky, flames of fire
and then black sticky rain
falling, falling on trees, on flowers, on rooftops,
on people, the world turning so black
it could not be washed off.

4

...Somewhere slow
poetry is being tender with its alphabet.
Don McKay, "A Morning Song"

Outside my house the morning sun spills,
gilded ripples across the bay.
The cranes stilt across the mudflats.

I wonder what they know, what we have lost,
these birds that mate for life.
Sometimes in the shallow waters of these wetlands,
the cranes dance,
sending waves flying, a language of ancient memories,

a language that teaches us that after grief, it is possible
to love again,
a music we have forgotten, such sheer joy.

When the cranes lift in ascent, cathedrals of wind
rise in their wingbones,
estuaries of morning light lifting across continents,
a white front of radiance,
their cries like clouds of desire.

After, in the presence of still waters,
you can rest in the white light, in the grace of wings.

Psalm for the Beloved

At the moment our bloods cease to mingle
at the instant of retreat of blood, skin, pulse
clock gears begin to grind and tick
sands pour from hourglasses
dust settles in every corner
chips fly from our bones
the magnolia's pink molts into brown.

In the scent of decay
I will hold you in stillness.
Do not let go of my hand.

Benediction

Because hands afraid of loss are the only hands for love.
                                        Yehuda Amichai

Wittgenstein writes that when the eye beholds beauty,
                              the hand wants to paint it.

I want to paint you, to write you, commit you to ink,
                              indigo-blue scrolled with blood
like pillowbooks of Japanese court women.

In the cradle of your hands
                    lies the grave of my mouth.
Your hands have rebuilt me.
You have hammered together the hinges of my ruined bones.

Your hands make early flowers of things.
Many forms of tenderness bloom in your palms.

Your hands wrench open the history I bear.
My black vault is unlatched for you to enter.

Let me begin every day like this,
                    in these first hours
grief lifted in your dawn-soaked hands.

Notes to Open the Memory Chamber

night ghosts
fragrance of peonies
decay of magnolia blossoms
heated swirl of cognac in my throat
the names and addresses of the dead in my book
ash on my tongue
gunfire
rivers of blood
children watching executions in soccer fields
women stoned for unborn babies
my wild patience burning
a fire in every room, every century
revolution
four winds of the heart
sweet, bitter poetry
a jewel for your perfect ear
testament
your sweet mouth

Crossing Boundary

for Suzanne Northcott

It was a crow you saw the night your lover died.
And for many nights after, the crow hovering
                     on the edge, that line between life and death
                     a boundary you imagine again and again
and then in the bones of your hands as they etch those smoke
lines across your canvases
those lines that haunt us, light and dark, claw and brush of wingbeats
                     luna moths crashing against screen doors,
                 rose petals drifting spent to the ground.

You told me the story   how he hung himself off a bridge with a rope,
how it took the police days to find his body, but you knew he was dead,
this man who once made you luminous.
How you once believed that love was in every repetition,
                         every small return,
night after night, gathered like black birds on a wire
and crows in alderwood
                their roosts like lanterns in the long shadows.
Every thin want could bloom in this, when fingers brush at some pulse
                      and you are gone with it.

Every story of love is like this, contained in a flicker of muscle,
memories in the press of garlic over a steaming pot of soup, a wine glass,
                          and always danger of the dark moment
when it all ceases to matter or make sense and it seems easier to take the edge
of the world, stand at that line and step over into the place your
                                              heart cannot reach.

When you tell   you no longer weep.
In the long years after his death you turn to
                                        paints and canvases
your strong hands flying across landscapes and the wings of crows
and everywhere that boundary line gleams.

Code

Nightfall.
Lights are extinguished
                              across the city.
Couples spoon together in
drugged sleep. The world blurs
                              to dream.

The sky is thunder and lightning
brilliantly open then dissolving
dark into itself.

I lie awake.
The long awaited prose
                              of your body
keeps me reading
re-reading.

You are the flammable pages I have
                              fallen against
venation of limbs
bolt of collarbone

name of your name
written without another's

astonished at my hunger.

Code Blue: A Fable

You would see yourself as if in the pages of a novel,
your own story beginning in the first sentence
                              hesitant, uncertain, without the end.

Semi-dark. The setting—a hospital.
You can read the red pulse of machines, the exit signs.
You are with a lover whose desire matches yours,
who won't wait a moment longer to peel back the hospital corners
drop your clothes in a tangle to the floor
                              and you find yourself in an emergency room
leaving a stain or two to prove that nothing like this
could ever be immaculate even though Christ is uttered
from your lips Oh Christ and both of you having died and
gone to heaven and now breathing steadily once again.

Somewhere, a woman is writing a poem

Somewhere, a woman is writing a poem
in the twilight hours of history, lavender turning to ash,
as time spills over and the moon unfurls her white-pitched fever in
the songs of jasmine winds. The young woman I was climbs the
stairs, the moon's pale alphabet filling her. She tucks her child into
bed, bends over her desk in the yellow lamplight, frees her hand
to write, breaking through the page like that Dorothea Tanning
painting where the artist's hand gashes through the canvas, fingers and
wrist plunged to the bone. She writes a dark, erotic psalm, an elegy,
a poem to grow old in, a poem to die in.

Somewhere, a woman is writing a poem,
as she gives away the clothes of her dead loved ones,
stretching crumpled wings, her words rise liquid in the air,
rosaries of prayer for the dying children, for the ones who
have disappeared, the *desaparecido*, and for the ones who
have been murdered. She writes through the taste of fear and
rage and fury. She writes in milk and blood, her ink fierce and
iridescent, rooted in love. Somewhere, a woman who thought
she could say nothing is writing a poem and she will sing forever,
blooming in the dark madness of the world.

Let Me Tell You of The Sacred

She is there in my dreams
the child made of our holiest hours.

The child you and I will never have.

If the sacred could speak for itself
it would be whispered through her
in the way we would wake her

in her halo of dark curls

in her hand outstretched to yours.

Berceuse

The sun has unhinged itself
to the moon's milk light
on my dreaming girl
                  in the ribcage of her cradle

I rock her and the universe loses its centre
                         to the incisions of dreams.
My word-bound eyes offer a scorched vigilance
each thing wrenched from its own darkness.

Doubt is a garment I dare not wear
                  in the face of this child
her tender skull preparing for the world
                  in cloud chambers
her calm a miracle against the way she entered
                              the world
torn from my body by iron hands.

This is the zone of the wages of love
                  no justice apparent
courtroom gavel hammered down
no one in the witness stand.

How do I belong to all this
from the unfettered moment
           my skin burning under your father's hands
to our daily vanishings and dawnings.

You are the world's sound
           against my flesh
a breaking radiance loosed from your
light-soaked fingers
           the clench of your fist redolent
with strange joy and love and damage.

Therefore

You, incommensurate, therefore
                                    the hours shine.
You are a concordance of number, voice,
person and place. Though your eyes waste
away in grief, feel the arm that would hold
you up so you will not slip. You are the perpetual
bridegroom coming out of the chamber. Heart's
desire will always honey you, innocent of rebuke
and transgression.

You are delivered over and over.

You are poured out like water.
Your heart of wax has melted at the brink of
death. Assemblies of the wicked have pierced
you. Count all your bones and you will find a
dwelling place, bed of green, home of still waters
as you fall from the sky, mouth full of lilies.

You have come to be my every day, my night.

Home is nowhere, therefore we become
a kind of dwell and welcome, free from any
eden we could name.

Amas Veritas

Night after night, you are there in your house
                          sitting in darkness on a tender evening.
You drink your acid sweet coffee, cigarette dangling
an old melody coiling around your fingers,
the drip of the faucet, the bath, the furnishings
your velvet safety from the day's bitterness.

———

Fear is always your first word.
You hear it in the wind.
The weight of love grows soft with despair.

Your ghosts are between us.
You will die from the false song
                  in the full sentence of the fugue.
Bury ghosts in the woods
                  dig their graves at the crossroads.

The moon will deliver us from evil
                        or from love.

———

We survive until morning.
Sleep covers your face soaked with light.
In the room's heavy scent I watch your breathing.

Remember the warm suspended darkness,
                              cool dusks,
your flesh made sweet by the thick-walled
chambers of your mother's heart.

I am with you at your moment of waking
                  lodged between tooth and tongue.

We do not choose to love.
It breaks us and we obey.

The Poetry of Things

In the click of the camera, the
room is stilled in the aperture of memory.
The room no longer exists and nothing
is the same, but objects claim us with
each familiar glistening.

The curve of this bowl, heat from
the hands that made it. The breath of
clay and burnished sheen of copper.

The strand of pearls, the 21st birthday, the
wedding trousseau, the lover's gift still warm
from the clasp of the throat.

The ring, the locket, the strand of hair,
the broken and then mended heart.

Worn-out sneakers, the teenager's
basketball, gardener's gloves. The straw
hat, the sun-warmed day.

The white shirt, the office day
undone. The sweater, elbows worn
soft. Bathrobe wrapped against the night.

Evening shoes, bottles of scent,
tangle of stockings and bra. The cut-glass

goblet, ruby sip of wine. The nightgown,
the shoulders kissed.

Leather suitcases. Trains and journeys,
safaris and pilgrimages.

Easels and paints, the trace of
alizarin crimson.

Coffee cups, bitter-sweet
espresso.

The vase of flowers, full-blown
petals of parrot tulips.

The slim volumes of poetry, thumb-worn
pages yellowing.

Baby shoes, silver cups and rattles,
hair ribbons, girls' dresses, smocked and
sashed, the graduation gown
lavender sheer.

Somewhere an infant cries, the mouth
rooting for the nipple, draws her mother's
milk. A little girl runs, her red Mary Janes
tapping pavement music.

Nothing is as it was.
In the photograph, these
old rooms, our forgotten bodies there,
the necessities of ritual contained
the instants sad and beautiful of
things human still warm with print of
fingertips and flesh
luminous and beloved.

Memento Mori

Estelle unbuttons her blouse, lays my
hand on the jagged scar where her breast
used to be. She wants me to tell her she is
still beautiful.

I feel her heart beneath the ribbed wall
milk-veined softness knifed into a cavern.
She tells me her husband has not been able
to look at it yet, this place on a woman's body,
nuzzled and suckled and cupped by infants
and lovers.

Her gesture recalls my
first lover, his teenage body, long six foot
stretch, lean limbs, every rib visible, the
surgical scar after the mending of a collapsed
lung. I used to breathe into that curved mark
above his heart, lay my head against its pulse.

Three decades later, I realize my lover
has that same six foot stretch of bones, that
tender ribcage.

How we return, full cycle, to first love.
While ashes that rise meet ashes that fall
we become the world for a while, the rose
of each lung blooming inside.

All this contained in the memory of my hand
on Estelle's heart, her absent breast, sweet flesh
excised into terrible beauty. I tell her she is beautiful,
despite her husband's averted gaze, that she will continue
to be loved.

It cannot be otherwise.
For her mother has named her with human faith.
Estelle, her name a star.

Postscript

for my daughter who would be my eulogist

Dearest Rachel

Last night you had a dream. It was my funeral.
You were reading my eulogy. You spoke of my
perpetual claim that any day was a good day to die.

There is nothing definitive to be said of the dead.
But I have some requests for your future script my darling.

Tell those who are gathered that I have loved and
I have been beloved.

You do not need to speak of virtue or morals. You may
wish to say I endured suffering but that I believed my bruises
to be pale beside the wounds of history.

Tell them that I loved my companions most of all.
You have been one of them who gave me a better way to
journey alone.

Spread my ashes into the blue waters of the bay I have loved,
for there, on the wings of cranes, in the embrace of the delta
and its wetlands, it is always morning.

P.S.

You may have:
my black dress
my red shoes
my pearls
my hats and suitcases
my inks and pens
my books and manuscripts.
Make of these things a breathing archive.
Write yourself into every century.
Find me again and again as one with whom
faith could be kept.

Slow Burn

1

One of my students brings her infant son to class.
As I hold him I am reminded how sweet it feels to
        carry a child who still hasn't lost the smell of angel dust.

How the body longs to decay.
                Springtime seeps out of me, relentless
                      terminal pull. My life, this garment
                          which is on fire.

———————

The song keeps turning over and over again,
                lullaby and fugue
Nothing changes through the decades.
                Each time, we adjust our hearts.

Prosodies come and go
            move in and out of fashion.
And every spring is a scorched season
                of slow fire,
                    new buds stung by rain
Droplets on the cowls of crocuses announce
                reluctance.

How we harden and burn
            as the sun rises and night shrugs.

———

You still move me
        in this hard season.

I still find redemption in your mouth, in your hands.

———

Word-drunk. Memento scrivi.

There is no secret contingency. We rearrange, describe anew the
        small, mortal things.

This single body making a tiny garment, my flesh-dress
        gathering the past against itself.
Making an otherwise.

We are our final vocabulary
        and how we use it.
What we have learned in the dark: lovemaking that is a form of prayer.
The simple truth of it. The sounds in our throats when we are most alive.
The going down on all fours. Love that renders us howling, mewling,
        the animal whelps of recognition.

———

In the end the world is a language we never quite understand.
Poets jot down the alphabets of everyday.
                    All speech pulls us toward the infinite.
History threatens to swallow us
                    year after year.

————————

2

Springtime along the wetlands of Iraq, on the banks of the Tigris
and Euphrates rivers.
Thousands of white storks migrate in the path of F15 bombers,
                    their nesting grounds blasted apart.

By the roadside, a five year old girl in her gold and orange dress.
Her dead body beside the bridge.
A young American soldier holds her in his arms,
            tries to bury her in the shallow grave of Iraqi dirt.

Leave her he is told by his superior *There is no time for this.*

And so she is left there, the earth beginning to ripen into the
meaning of murder
            sweet girl in her perfect dress.

On these days when something monstrous flashes across your eyes
vision, newspaper headline, snapshot, nightmare of a child dying
Rise at dawn to beg a merciless God to take away these images.
Listen to your own deepest breath. Go down on your knees.
Taste everything.

Give us this day the slant of sunlight. Hold the rain in your hands.

Hold still   hold still

––––––––––

3

Take off your traveling clothes.
                        Set down your bags.

Lay your head upon me. You are home.
My robe is lined with crimson silk for you. Love will kill us.
Love will save us.
                  Love and the words from beneath the earth

As God knees us to the ground
                  tempts us to stop-out

Remember   battle of the red cells   shattered fragments of hell
                prayer smoke wreckage   starred flesh

Whir of monarch butterflies, orange-gold dust of thousands of wings.

Listen to the earth's prayer which has the perfume of newborns.

The right word can send you breathless.

Everything is speaking and singing. We are here.

This life. Long, slow burn of a struck match.

Strange Fruit

for Luz Minero

Sun streaming across classroom desks.
Textbooks splayed open. I have assigned a quote from the text,
asking for response to the list of qualities essential for
the effective teacher of literature. The book tells my
students that they must be risk-takers, subversive, that
they must read gladly and openly, for this is their best
hope of introducing others to literature. We use the
book's language, critical thinking, socio-political thought,
the English teacher as subversive.

Chalk dust powders my hands, the walls echo loud
chatter until Luz reads her response:
*During the civil war in El Salvador in the 1980s it was not
unusual to find teachers of literature hanging from trees.*
The room weeps. My spine slips, throat closes.
In this classroom, the dark fields of history loom,
edgelit with outrage and the knowledge that language
is always culpable.

Textbooks are momentarily discarded.

The Scent of Poppies

after reading the Vancouver Sun, July 6, 1999

In my garden, the poppies have bloomed. Petals fall scarlet tissue to the ground. I gather the light of these flowers, watch my daughters run to the beach, their long limbs flying down the road to the sea's embrace.

I read the newspaper headline *Scent of poppies, stench of death.* The story is of a land dismembering itself. Outside Kosovo's capital Pristina is the Road to Leskovac, Makovac, Yugoslavia. Look closer. Call it Highway to Hell. Ethnic Albanians return home along this country road, the air reeking with the stench of death from houses, from mass graves in fallow fields overgrown with wild flowers. Fields of poppies.

Here is a living room. Inside, a shroud of ashes shaped like the body of a man who was rolled in blankets and burned alive. Here the wind blows music through walls punctured with bullet holes, where Serbian men executed men while they kneeled, their words of prayer caught in the stopped pulse of the world.

Here is the house used as a chamber of rape. On the floor dozens of buttons ripped from clothes, bloody blankets, women's underwear.

Here are the cows, slaughtered by machine gun, deliberate hands, pistol chambers triggering bullets through their heads. Their carcasses lie among the fields of flowers, brilliant wounds of poppies, scent of rotting flesh mingling with the perfume of crushed lavender.

Here is the black quartz watch in the mass grave, still ticking next to the sleeve of the man who once wore it. And everywhere in the villages under skies full of pitch and smoke, women bury their men, fathers, husbands, lovers, sons, women's labour rinsing away the fetid stench, scrubbing, scrubbing.

In my garden, my fingers blacken with the newsprint. I hear my daughters laughing. The charred utterings of poets.

The poppies tremble.

Cartography

I once believed that one word had the
power to change things, that language
was a skin we could inhabit. Now I know
poems are theories, carving memory
into the long spine of history. We are
caught in the throat, voicing the hours.

The poet's exile is pure sound at the
scarred edges of the world's body.

Country, nation, history. I am changing the
story. My hand is moving across your page and
it is in the mapping of your bones and sinews that
I find the words: *grief, love, beauty, testament.*
Your mouth yields the vermilion fruit of the word
home. Let me die here.

Theology

This is always what it comes to.

The decision to understand *significance*.

How love's meaning is held in that moment
> full of terror, rage, grief, tenderness, trust,

that round, full moment undeniable
> like the mouth closed on the sweetness of an orange

like the flesh kissed again and again in the warm falling rain.

This is it   held out to you for the taking.

> Accidental. Raw as faith.

Retablos

For the girl with braces on her teeth, a ragdoll in her arms,
a smile of her own, a grin the size of this room.

For the woman whose mind paces in fever in its bone cage,
a circuitry of prayers, hymnals as salve.

For the prayerbook, someone to thumb it open every day.

For the insomniac,
the lullaby of all that flows, rivers, a woman's blood.

For the one who is stunned at the power of his own rage
an admittance of singing, a night without the thickness of terror.

For the mother and father of the murdered child,
a city that would lay her bones to rest, a dreamless sleep.

For the ones whose ribcages have fallen, ashes rising to meet dust,
the arms of the world for a little while.

For the girl in Tijuana who asked for a dollar in exchange for taking
her photograph,
the sweetness of raspberries.

For the imprisoned Cuban poet who was made to eat her own words,
manifesto stuffed down her throat,
books and books of her poems, hardbound and glossy jacketed
on the shelves of every bookstore and library and school of the world.

For the woman who weeps the way one weeps after making love
with a lover she has grown old with,
when loss feels most certain,
eyes with light enough to read the braille of her lover's bones
breaking inside her.

For the girl who cuts herself,
the will to dance, a bouquet of peonies for her burning palms.

Nothing is lost unless we make it so.
For the one who has chosen to make it so,
my kiss upon your torn wings, the thorn of your heart.

Claim

All she did was read. This left a commotion in her wake. Reading as faith. Book as talisman. Startled breath. Childhood sets of golden books. Nursery of stars. Winken, Blinken and Nod. Kipling has a theory about how the alphabet came to be. *Cahiers d'exercices.* Lined notebook with pink margin. Faint blue lines of sans serif. Vanish through a rabbit hole, a looking glass, a wardrobe. Take a blessing from the lion. Find a page that does not tear the retina. Paul Éluard's love poems. Poems that enter like slivers of glass. In the burned libraries everything is winged and dreaming. *Soirs volés. Nuits blanches.* We are not all born with grace. A manifesto of stars is necessary. Words unfurling on prayer flags. Cicero's memory palaces. Reading Yehuda Amichai. *Open Closed Open. The language of love and tea with roasted almonds.* After Auschwitz, no theology. *The touch of longing is everywhere.* Click of ruby heels. The letter that begins in honesty Dearest Beloved. After Rwanda, no language. Poem that temples grief. Stone of witness. Tablet of amen and love. The breath of Rappaccini's daughter a fatal kiss. In the ruined garden stand in the shadow of the scar. Her hands busied by daylight. Schopenhauer approves of art. The experience of art constitutes cessation of the will: beauty wipes the slate clean. The nape of her neck bent over the page. The heart is the toughest part of the body. Tenderness is in the hands. Repair. After a requiem begin to hear the noise of the world again. Door opening as the palm of the eye. A poetry of shine.

Notes

Saccade

Reference to "Didn't Leave Nobody But the Baby." The lyrics are from a gospel lullaby performed by Emily Harris, Alison Kraus and Gillian Welch on the soundtrack of Joel and Ethan Coen's 2000 film "O Brother, Where Art Thou," Mercury Records 2000.

Last lines of the second to last stanza are echoes of lines in Robert Creeley's poem "The Rain." Creeley writes: "Be for me, like rain,... Be wet/with a decent happiness." The poem appears in *For Love: Poems 1950-1969*. New York: Scribners, 1962, p.190.

Augustinian Heart

Italicized line in this poem and in the epigraph of the book is from Augustine's Confessions 10, 27.

Lector in Fabula

Title borrowed from Umberto Eco's book *Lector in Fabula* translated as *The Reader in the Story.*

The Reader

Gerhard Richter's painting "Lesende" (Reader) is held in the permanent collection of The San Francisco Museum of Modern Art. Oil on linen, 28.5 "x 40.13" (72.39 cm.x 101.92 cm.).

Reading Like a Girl :3

Lines from the Warner's advertisement for the Merry Widow corset are from *Ladies Home Journal,* September 1955.

Soja

Lyrics for "Jamaica Farewell" are by Harry Belafonte from the RCA recording, *Calypso*, 1956, LPM-124S.

Lyrics for "Soja Raj Kumari" are from a Hindi song written by Kundan Lal Saigal and featured in the score of a 1940 Bollywood film titled "Zindagi."

The Lost Language of Cranes

The title of this poem was inspired by David Leavitt's novel of the same title.

Epigraph by Peter Schwenger is from *Letter Bomb. Nuclear Holocaust and The Exploding Word.* John Hopkins University Press, 1992. Epigraph by Carolyn Forché is from "The Garden of Shukkei-en," in *The Angel of History,* New York: HarperCollins, 1994. Epigraph by Don McKay is from *Birding, or desire.* Toronto: McLelland & Stewart, 1983.

Hibakusha: The term *hibakusha* refers to survivors of the Atomic Bomb. Epigraph by Isao Kita and segments of this poem are informed by the testimonies collected and videotaped by the Hiroshima Peace and Culture Foundation to commemorate the International Year of Peace in 1986.

Excerpts referring to Sadako Sasaki's mother, Fujiko Sasaki, are based on a letter titled, "Come Back to Me Sadako," from *Record of Atomic Bombs in Japan* by Seishi Toyota, Nihon Tosho Center, 1991.

Benediction

Epigraph by Yehuda Amichai is from "I Foretell the Days of Yore" (Section 6) in *Open, Closed, Open.* New York: Harcourt Brace, 2000.

Somewhere a woman is writing a poem

This poem is for The 2am Collective and for Gene Diaz and Martha McKenna.

The Scent of Poppies

The line "Scent of poppies, stench of death" is from the title of an article by Valerie Reitman in the Vancouver Sun, Tuesday, July 6, 1999.

Acknowledgments

I would like to extend my grateful acknowledgment to The Ontario Arts Council for the generous support of a Works in Progress Grant.

My thanks to Mary Engel, daughter of photographer Ruth Orkin, for her permission to use the cover photograph by Ruth Orkin titled "Comic Book Readers" New York 1947. Reprinted with permission of the Estate of Ruth Orkin.

Thanks to Marty Gervais, publisher of Black Moss Press, whose enthusiasm, encouragement and faith brought these poems together in book form.

My thanks and gratitude to Christopher Doda for his astute and thoughtful responses to poems and for editing suggestions.

Thanks also to my editor with Black Moss Press, John B. Lee, for his remarkable skills, intelligence and integrity, gifts that helped shape this manuscript.

Special thanks to Joe Paczuski for his loving support, contributions and many acts of generosity.

Many others in my community of writers and friends have contributed in various ways to the shaping of this book. I will take this occasion to thank Denis DeClerck, Barry Dempster, Pier Giorgio DiCicco, Suzanne Northcott, Damiano Pietropaolo, Goran Simic, Priscila Uppal and Darryl Whetter.

My grateful acknowledgement and thanks to Luciano Iacobelli, publisher of LyricalMyrical Press for publishing a selection of these poems in *The Blue Hour* (limited edition chapbook with art by Suzanne Northcott).

Photo: Kristina Vaca

Rishma Dunlop was born in India and was raised in Ottawa and Beaconsfield, Quebec. She is a poet and fiction writer whose work has won awards and has been published widely in books, journals and anthologies, nationally and internationally. She was a finalist for the 1998 CBC/Saturday Night Canada Council Literary Award for poetry and the recipient of the Emily Dickinson Award in 2003. Her previous books of poetry are: *Boundary Bay* (Staccato 2000), *The Body of My Garden* (Mansfield Press 2002), *The Blue Hour* (LyricalMyrical Press, 2004). She currently lives in Toronto where she is a professor of Literary Studies in the Faculty of Education at York University.